#1

MYSTERIES ON ZOO LANE

Meet the Crew at the Zoo

Patricia Reilly Giff

illustrated by
Abby Carter

HOLIDAY HOUSE · NEW YORK

Text copyright © 2020 by Patricia Reilly Giff

Art copyright © 2020 by Abby Carter

All Rights Reserved

HOLIDAY HOUSE is registered in the U.S. Patent and Trademark Office.

Printed and bound in January 2021 at Maple Press, York, PA, USA.

www.holidayhouse.com

First Edition

3 5 7 9 10 8 6 4 2

Library of Congress Cataloging-in-Publication Data

Names: Giff, Patricia Reilly, author. | Carter, Abby, illustrator.

Title: Meet the crew at the zoo / by Patricia Reilly Giff ; illustrated by Abby Carter.

Description: First edition. | New York : Holiday House, [2020]

Series: Mysteries on Zoo Lane ; book 1 | Audience: Ages 7 and up.

Audience: Grades 2-3. | Summary: Luke is unhappy about leaving his home and
abuelo when his father takes a job at a New York zoo, but soon he has new friends
and a mystery to solve. Includes facts about zoo animals and wildlife.

Identifiers: LCCN 2019029201 ISBN 9780823446667 (hardcover)

Subjects: CYAC: Zoos—Fiction. | Moving, Household—Fiction.

Family life—Fiction. Friendship—Fiction. | Zoo animals—Fiction.

Mystery and detective stories. | Classification: LCC PZ7.G3626 Mc 2020

DDC [Fic]—dc23 | LC record available at https://lccn.loc.gov/2019029201

ISBN: 978-0-8234-4666-7 (hardcover)

ISBN: 978-0-8234-4850-0 (paperback)

ISBN: 978-0-8234-4815-9 (ebook)

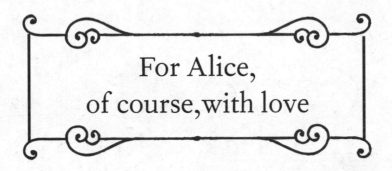

For Alice,
of course, with love

CHAPTER 1

THE plane roared to a stop. Luke's throat burned. He told himself he was too old to cry.

Dad was talking. "You'll love this place with its new zoo, Luke. Animals will too."

Dad waved his arms around. "Their spaces will be large. They'll look like their homes in the wild. And their food will taste just right."

Luke tried to nod. The animals might be happy here. But would he?

If only they were back with his abuelo, near the zoo in Florida.

Abuelo had looked so sad when they left.

Dad knew what Luke was thinking. "I'm really sorry. But I'll be the zoo doctor here."

Luke wanted to say, you were the zoo doctor in Florida. And I had friends. I had Abuelo.

Dad patted Luke's arm. "We're home in New York now."

"Home," Mom echoed.

Luke had been born in New York. But he hardly remembered it.

"You may not be happy at first," Dad said. "But you'll see."

Mom put her arms around Luke and his five-year-old sister, Benita, while they waited for their bags.

It was almost night. Luke tried not to yawn.

A taxi came next. It drove them from one street to another.

Luke peered out the window.

The taxi was stopping . . . at a falling-down house on Zoo Lane.

Blue paint had chipped off the walls.

In Abuelo's house, the paint stayed where it belonged. A nice green color.

Luke listened to Benita sing as they went up the walk. She was always singing. "This place looks like it might be horrible. At least I think so."

Luke swallowed. She might be right.

CHAPTER 2

INSIDE, they rushed to the window.

"It's too dark to see out there," Benita said.

"We'll see it tomorrow," Dad said.

He leaned over Luke's shoulder. "Aren't we lucky! The zoo begins in the back of our house. Abuelo would have loved it."

Luke thought of his grandfather with his white beard and mustache.

Abuelo worked at the Florida zoo. He knew all about giraffes and camels and kangaroos.

He loved tigers too. How

worried he looked when he said they were "endangered."

It was the first time Luke had heard that word. He stumbled over it: "endangered."

Abuelo had shaken his head. "The wild animals' forests are farms now, and trees are cut down for wood. But worse is the illegal poaching."

Luke frowned. Hadn't he heard those words before? Weren't they about killing wild animals for fur and feathers, for meat and even medicines?

Abuelo had said, "We need

zoos to help. How terrible if the animals were gone."

"Time for bed," Mom said.

Bed in this new house!

Luke passed an empty bedroom in the hall. It was dark. Scary.

He could hardly see anything in his room either.

He threw on his pajamas and dived into bed.

The closet door was open.

A place for something to hide!

He'd read about a monster with claws. It was a made-up story for fun.

But still . . .

In bed, he heard a roar.

"Yeow!" He pulled the quilt over his head. He slid the pillow on top.

He could hardly breathe.

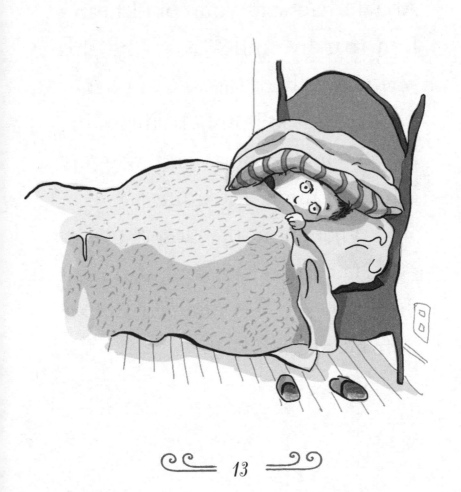

"It's only a lion," Benita sang from her bedroom.

Luke crossed his fingers. "I wasn't afraid."

Abuelo had said you could hear a lion roar five miles away. But this one was only in the zoo out back.

It was too hot! Luke threw the pillow on the floor and wiggled out from under the quilt.

What about the closet?

He jumped up and slammed the door shut. He dragged a chair in front of it.

Safe!

He went back to bed. What a terrible place this was.

If only he weren't afraid of the dark.

Did he say it aloud?

"Count the animals," Benita sang. "You'll fall asleep."

Good idea.

"Tigers," he began. "Lions, seals, giraffes . . ."

CHAPTER 3

IT was morning.

"We have to hurry," Dad said. He was on his way to the zoo. "A black spider monkey might be born today."

Luke threw on his jeans. He was going too. Soon he'd begin to help.

At the stove, Mom fried bananas. She'd buttered toast to go with them.

Luke finished breakfast in three minutes. But Dad was already on his way.

Luke shoved a piece of toast in his pocket.

"What a mess," Benita said.

Did she ever mind her business? At least she'd forgotten to sing. He grinned at her.

Outside, he caught up with Dad. They went through the iron zoo gates.

Next they circled a pond. A

green flag flew in front: TORTOISE TOWN.

"Imagine," Dad told him. "Those giant tortoises lay eggs as big as tennis balls."

Abuelo had told him that too.

He'd said they could live almost two hundred years.

They kept going. Keepers were

feeding the animals. Some ate meat. Some had greens. Some even ate mice.

Poor mice!

Dad unlocked the door to a white building: THE BABY ZOO HOUSE.

"Want to look around outside?" he asked. "There'll be plenty of time for you to help me."

"Sure." Luke wandered down a path. Tree branches met over his head. A squirrel chittered somewhere.

"Don't miss the giant anteater," a woman said. She was wearing a raincoat.

A raincoat on this hot sunny day?

She must have known what he was thinking.

"I keep the ponds clean." She grinned at him.

He grinned back.

"Anteaters are my favorites," she said. "I talk to schoolchildren about them."

Luke nodded.

"They're great swimmers," the woman said, waving her arms around. "They use their long snouts as snorkels."

"Really?"

"Everyone calls me Nana-Next-Door," she said.

"Really," he said again.

"I live next door to the zoo," she said. "I even live next door to you."

Luke closed his mouth before he could say "really" again.

He watched as Nana cleaned around the edge of the pond.

He looked along the path. A boy was sweeping toward him.

Dust rose in the air.

Luke bent over sneezing.

The boy raised his shoulders.

Was he sorry? Luke couldn't tell.

A box lay half hidden in the bushes.

Luke reached for it. So did the boy. They rolled on the path.

"Hey," Luke yelled.

The boy yelled "hey" too.

Was he friendly? Maybe not.

Were the kids terrible here?

CHAPTER 4

Wrong!

"Sorry." The boy let go of the box.

Luke let go too.

"Are you a new kid?" The boy didn't wait for an answer. "I'm an old kid, Mitchell. I've always lived here."

Luke nodded. "I'm Luke, named for my grandfather. Almost. His name is Lukas."

"Let's see what's in the box," Mitchell said.

A peacock swept past. He fanned out his blue and gold

feathers. They stopped to watch.

Then they opened the box,

which had a zebra-striped cover.

Inside was a green collar. Luke's favorite color.

The collar was too small for a jaguar, too big for a black spider monkey.

The best part was a dollar bill,

never mind that it was old and crinkled.

A note was stuck to it. FOR FOOD THE FIRST DAY.

A girl went by, a cat in her arms.

Luke held up the box. "Yours?" he called.

"No, sorry," the girl said.

"That's Tori," Mitchell told him.

But then Dad was calling. "Luke?"

The black spider monkey must have been born.

Luke was ready to run. "My

father wants me." But what about the box? "Maybe we could find out whose it is."

"Wait, I can't help," Mitchell said. "Sorry. I'm going to Zoo Camp for a week. See you when I get back."

"See you." Luke would take the box. Maybe he could find the owner.

"Get some of the kids to help," Mitchell said.

"All right." He didn't want to say that the only kid he knew was his five-year-old sister.

Mitchell called back, "Just watch out for Alex. He never stops talking."

CHAPTER 5

LUKE opened the Baby Zoo House door. He was out of breath.

Dad smiled. "Look."

The mother black spider monkey was behind a glass door. A baby was wrapped around her middle.

Luke leaned forward.

He saw a tiny head and closed eyes.

"The mom looks like a spider when she holds on to branches," Dad said. "She has long legs, a long tail. They go in different directions."

She could grab the closet monster with one leg. She'd slam the door with her tail.

"Can you train a black spider monkey?" he asked.

Dad shook his head. "No. And really important, Luke: Wild animals are never meant to be pets."

He nodded. Dad had said that over and over.

Luke saw another door. STAY OUT, the sign said.

"What's in there?" he asked.

Dad didn't answer. He looked at his watch. "The zoo is opening."

Luke went outside. People were walking up the path.

Kids were standing near Nana-Next-Door. She was talking about anteaters.

"No teeth," she said, "but

sticky tongues.
They scoop up
thousands of ants
every day."

She saw Luke and
waved.

He waved back. Then
he dusted off the zebra box with
his elbow.

He thought of Mitchell.

A new friend?

But he'd be gone for ... Luke
couldn't remember how long.

What good was that?

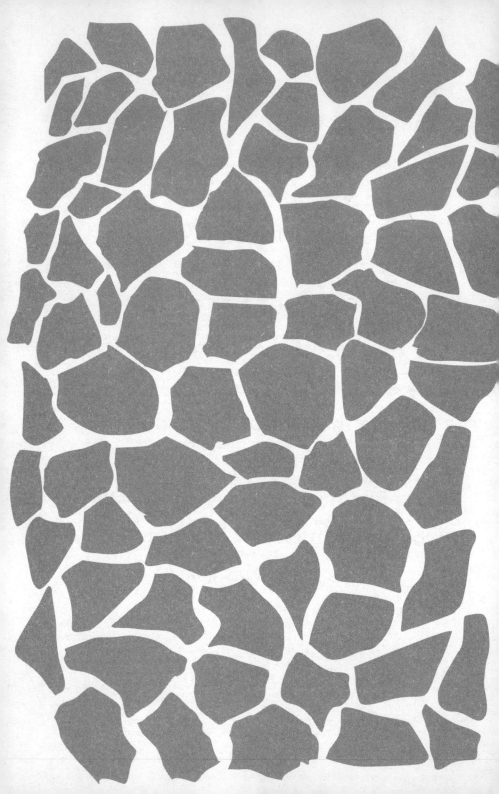

CHAPTER 6

AT Tapir Town, Luke sank down on a bench.

The tapirs were huge. Abuelo had said they weighed hundreds of pounds.

One of them raised its snout; it curled its lip.

Was it making a face at him?

He curled his lip too, just for fun.

There was a shadow next to him.

Luke looked up. A boy stood there. His jeans had mud on the knees. His sneakers were filthy.

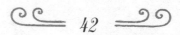

"Hey." The boy gave the box a rap. "What do you have there?"

He left a handprint of dirt.

Luke held the box tighter.

The boy gripped his shoulder. "It might be mine. I had a box like that. I've looked all over . . ."

"What's inside?" Luke asked.

"I don't remember. It was a zebra box, though. I had it yesterday."

"Is your name Alex?" Luke asked.

"Right," said the boy. "It's not a great name. I couldn't spell the

whole thing at first: Alexander. The kids laughed . . ."

He was never going to stop talking. Luke nodded and hurried up the path.

"Wait," Alex called. "I'll tell you about . . ."

Luke crossed Zoo Lane.

Footsteps came behind him.

He climbed his front steps.

The door was locked.

He rang the bell and kept his finger on it.

At last Benita opened the door.

She stood on tiptoes to look over Luke's shoulder.

"Come on in," she said.

Was she talking to Alex?

CHAPTER 7

"HEY, Tori," Benita was saying.

Luke ducked inside. He looked back. It was the girl with the cat.

Alex was trotting across the lawn, going the other way.

"Where's the cat?" Luke asked.

"Home, slurping down my mom's miso soup."

She made slurping noises. Her teeth were covered with orange braces.

She touched the box with one finger. "Zebra stripes."

"It's not mine," Luke said.

Benita was talking at the same time. "Mom made cookies. Want one?"

Tori circled around him into the house.

She followed Benita down the hall.

"My friend David used to live here," Tori said. "You can see the whole zoo from the attic window."

In the kitchen, Benita held out a plate of cookies. They were mostly crumbs. "I ate a few."

She raised her shoulders. "I guess I ate a lot."

"I don't blame you." Tori scooped up a raisin. She looked toward the attic stairs. "It's cool up there."

Benita wiped her mouth. "Let's go."

Luke took the last crumb. Then he followed them up.

Heat blasted in the attic.

"I thought you said it was cool." Benita wiped her forehead.

"I meant *neat*," Tori said.

She was right. Luke could see

the zoo from the filthy window. All of it.

Alex was there, leaning against the fence. He was talking to somebody . . . or maybe one of the animals.

Tori pointed. "I love the jaguars. Their spots look like roses. I read that they're called rosettes."

Luke looked down at the jaguars. Dad was just beyond them in an empty field.

Three kids were looking at the jaguars too. They were eating popcorn.

"From zebra boxes!" he said.

the Blue Zoo Stand. Everything's blue. Ice cream, cotton candy. All except the boxes."

Luke dived down the attic stairs.

He raced to the Blue Zoo Stand.

CHAPTER 8

LUKE ran along the zoo path. He passed Dad in the field.

He circled around another field.

Tigers lay there. They stared at him with their great yellow eyes. One of them yawned.

Nana-Next-Door was watching them.

"Gorgeous, aren't they?" she said.

"My grandfather works at a zoo. He says that their stripes are like fingerprints. Every tiger is different."

Nana-Next-Door nodded. "If only your grandfather were here. He could talk to a group of kids with me."

"I wish he was here too," Luke said.

But he was wasting time. He began to run again.

He slid to a stop at the Blue Zoo Stand. Bins were filled with blue popcorn and cotton candy. The popcorn smelled great . . . or was it the cotton candy?

A teenaged boy leaned against the counter. He wore a Blue Zoo cap. OMAR was written across the front.

Omar's father was at the other end of the stand. He was scooping blue ice cream into a cup.

Omar leaned forward. "You're the new kid on Zoo Lane. Right?"

"I'm Luke. You live on Zoo Lane too?"

"Down at the end," Omar said. "Can I help you?"

"Is anyone looking for a zebra box?"

"Are you kidding?" Omar pointed to the litter basket.

Inside were dozens of boxes.

Some were crushed. Others had ice cream smears.

Luke shook his head. "It's a new box. It has a dollar inside."

Omar stared at him. "Sometimes I put money in a box. Maybe it's mine."

Alex wanted the box! And now Omar!

"What else was inside?" Luke asked.

Omar pushed his cap back. "I put junk in them." He stopped to think. "A Blue Zoo cookie?"

Luke shook his head.

"Maybe a pen."

"No."

"A dollar anyway," Omar said.

"I'll think about it," Luke said.

It was time for lunch.

All that popcorn was making him hungry.

"See you later," he told Omar.

He walked along the path.

He thought of Abuelo and the zoo in Florida.

They'd been in Florida for a year. But he'd made friends in two minutes.

He wouldn't be walking alone.

Dad was coming toward him.

"That field would be the perfect

place . . ." He stopped to take a
breath.

Luke waited.

". . . for giraffes."

Yes!

"There are plants with thorns,"
Dad said.

Luke knew that giraffes had
thick tongues and lips . . .

Thick enough to chew on
plants with thorns.

Abuelo was worried about the giraffes. Ana trees were being cut down. Giraffes couldn't eat their leaves anymore.

Dad must have been thinking the same thing. "Zoos have to help," he said.

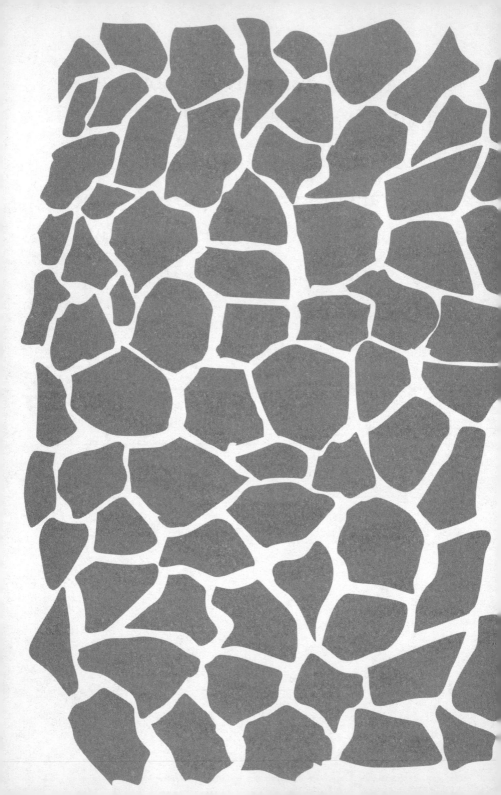

CHAPTER 9

THE next morning, Luke opened his eyes. Mom was standing in the doorway. "You might find a surprise here," she said.

"What surprise?"

"You'll have to see."

Then she was on her way to the kitchen.

Dad was calling. "Hurry, Luke. You have to see this."

Luke stumbled out of bed. He found a pair of shorts.

Benita was in the hall. "I forgot," she sang.

Luke waited.

She took a breath. "Tori's brother might be missing a zebra box," she said.

Another person! Luke nodded as he went past.

He and Dad didn't stop to eat. Mom gave them bottles of juice and muffins.

Luke brought the zebra box with him. But he wasn't thinking of that now.

He and Dad walked to a field that looked almost like a desert. "Meerkats," Dad said. "New to this new zoo."

"I don't see any animals." Luke bit into a blueberry muffin.

Dad put his hand on his shoulder. "Wait. They're still in their burrows."

Burrows? Was this Mom's surprise?

How could it be? Luke knew

that there were animals who dug holes at night. They'd sleep there until morning.

Dad nudged him. "Here they come."

A pile of them. Thirty? Forty?

They scampered around, searching for their own breakfast of insects, or maybe lizards.

All except one. It stood there looking up at the sky.

"A lookout for enemies," Dad said. "Eagles, maybe. Meerkats watch out for each other."

How lucky they were to have friends, Luke thought.

Dad patted his arm. "I'll see about a zoo that might send giraffes." He took the path to the office.

Luke took the last bite of muffin.

Then he went after Dad. He'd promised to help.

Inside, he lugged small evergreen trees into a birthing room. Dad left his computer and they carried in ferns and little trees. The room looked like a small jungle.

"Just what a puma mother wants when she has her babies," Dad said.

Luke looked around at the green room with its sweet smell.

Abuelo would have loved it.

Luke loved it.

But it was time to think about the zebra box.

Whose was it?

Alex's?

Tori's brother's?

Omar's?

Omar had all those zebra boxes at the Blue Zoo Stand.

Maybe he kept money in one. It would be easy to mix them up.

Luke hurried to the Blue Zoo Stand.

Omar was alone today. His mouth was filled with blue popcorn. He held out a handful.

"Have some," said Omar.

"Great popcorn." Luke slid the box across the counter. "I brought this back for you."

Omar reached under the counter. He pulled out another box and rattled it.

Luke looked inside. A pen. A couple of pennies. A dollar.

Omar grinned. Hs teeth were blue from popcorn. "My dad found mine. Thanks anyway."

Luke nodded. Who was next?

He sighed. Alex, he guessed.

He wandered down the lane.

He passed the petting zoo.

Alex was holding a rabbit in each arm. He was talking to them.

"Hey, Alex," he called.

CHAPTER 10

THAT night, Luke kept watching television. He hated to go up to his dark bedroom.

Mom looked at the clock. "It's late."

Benita had fallen asleep an hour ago. He had to go upstairs.

He carried the zebra box with him.

The box wasn't Alex's.

"Mine is filled with coins," Alex had said this morning. "I have a list of things to buy for school."

He said a lot more, but Luke couldn't remember all of it.

Luke put the box next to him on the night table. It had to be Tori's brother's.

He looked at Alex's handprint.

But something was underneath. Writing.

Why hadn't he seen it before?

He turned the box one way, and then another.

Right side up.

Upside down.

There were loops and dashes. Something was underlined.

None of it made sense. It was too much to think about tonight.

He knelt up in bed. The light over the Baby Zoo House was friendly.

Dad was working there tonight.

Luke began to count. "Black spider monkeys, jaguars, rhinos, meerkats."

And then it was morning again.

Benita was singing. "Poor dangerous giraffes . . ."

Luke grinned. "Not danger-ous," he called. "Endangered."

"I know that," Benita said. "I'm making up a song so people will help."

Downstairs, Luke heard Dad come into the kitchen. "A quick breakfast," he said. "I have to go back. Baby pumas were born last night."

He ate quickly and went out the back door.

Luke hurried too. He couldn't wait to see the pumas in the jungle they'd made.

Then he had to find Tori. He'd give her the box.

He headed for the Baby Zoo House. Dad waved through the window.

Footsteps came behind him.

He turned. Alex!

He nodded at Luke. "New babies!" he said. "Could I . . ."

"I guess so." Luke opened the door.

Alex slid in behind him. They

followed Dad down the hall and looked through a window.

"Neat jungle." Alex leaned close to the glass. "Someday I want to go on a safari . . ."

"Luke did most of it," Dad said.

Alex grinned at him. "Not bad!"

A great feeling filled Luke's chest.

"Where's the puma mom?" Luke asked. "And I don't see her cubs."

Alex grabbed Luke's elbow and pointed.

Ah. There was a spotted coat, blue eyes almost open.

He looked at Alex. "Neat," they said together.

They went back down the hall with Dad.

Luke bumped into the closed door. "What's in there, anyway?"

Dad smiled. "I'll open it when it's time."

Luke raised his shoulders.

So did Alex.

"See you," Luke told him.

It was time to find Tori.

CHAPTER 11

TORI was in her backyard. She was leaning over a picnic table reading. "There's a story about a jaguar. I think I heard it in school. She came out of the jungle to play with kids."

Even Abuelo probably didn't know that, Luke thought.

He waved the box. "It must be your brother's."

"He's in the house." Tori cupped her hands around her mouth. "Hey, Ken."

Ken banged open the screen door.

"I'm right in the middle of something."

Luke held out the zebra box.

"Mine's inside, thanks." Ken nodded at him and went inside.

Luke sank down at the table. He rested the box in front of him.

Tori pulled it toward her. "Can I look inside?"

"Sure. It's not mine."

She held everything up. Then she closed the box again.

She turned it on its side. "Hey, what's this? An L?

"Here's more." She squinted. "A handprint. It's hard to see."

Luke leaned forward.

"Wait," she said. "I think it says, 'See Dad.'"

Luke closed his eyes.

Had Dad left the box for him? Could that be?

It felt right.

It felt terrific.

He thought of the green collar.

It might be something that needed to be walked.

He couldn't wait to find out.

CHAPTER 12

LUKE rushed back to the zoo. He held the box in his hand.

"You found it." Dad smiled. "A perfect time. The door is ready to open. The babies are set to go."

Luke looked down the hall.

"Go ahead," Dad said.

Luke opened the door. A scruffy dog wagged her tail.

Two puppies rolled over next to her. One of them looked at him.

How small he was.

Luke sat on the floor. The puppy climbed on his lap.

This dog was his.

It had to be!

Dad was nodding. "One for you, one for Benita, and one for Mom and me."

The zoo door opened. Luke looked down the hall. It was Nana-Next-Door.

"Ah, Luke," she said. "You've seen the new pups. A neat surprise."

She reached in to touch the mother dog. "Perfect pets."

She winked at him. "Much better than zoo animals like tigers. They might eat you for dinner."

She tilted her head. "You wouldn't even be enough for a

meal. They can eat eighty-eight pounds at once.

Luke heard a crunch. His puppy was chewing on a tiny biscuit.

"That's just right for him," Nana said.

She waved goodbye and went down the hall.

Luke and Dad followed. Luke carried the puppy box home; Dad walked with the mother.

He grinned at Luke. "We'll have our own little zoo."

Mom was waiting for them. She was making ice cream sundaes.

"A celebration," she said. "For our new four."

Luke held up three fingers. "The mom and two pups."

Mom and Dad looked at each other.

"The giraffes are coming this week," Dad said. "And two Bengal tigers. We need an expert to help us with them."

Mom held up four fingers. "Three dogs and . . ."

"An expert," Dad added.

Luke felt his heart beating fast. Did he know who the expert was?

Dad was nodding.

Was it possible?

"Abuelo?"

"Of course," Mom said. "He'll teach us all so many things."

Benita began to sing. "My brother has tears in his eyes . . ."

Luke could hardly talk. He scooped up his puppy. He went upstairs.

Benita and Mom went with him.

Mom stopped at the empty bedroom.

A light was on. "It won't be empty anymore," she said. "So I've painted the walls."

"Pale green," Luke said. "Abuelo's favorite color."

Pictures were taped to the wall: giraffes, tigers, and Abuelo standing with Luke and Benita.

"Abuelo was lonesome without us," Mom said. "And we were lonesome for him."

Luke was having trouble talking again. He went down the hall with his puppy. He put her up on his bed.

The puppy was whimpering.

Luke couldn't be afraid anymore. The puppy needed him.

"You're going to be tough one

day," he said. "Tough as a tiger."

A great name for a puppy.

Tiger leaned closer.

What had Dad said? "You may not be happy at first. But . . . you'll see."

Luke said it aloud to Tiger.

He had friends now. Tori and Omar.

Mitchell would be home soon. And there was Alex, who never stopped talking . . .

And best of all, Abuelo.

Luke heard Benita singing. "I have a dog. Her name is Sweet Pea."

Sweet Pea? Wow.

Luke patted Tiger's head. "Let's count. Then we'll fall asleep."

"Elephants, hippos, jaguars."

Tiger closed his eyes.

"Pumas . . ."

Luke closed his eyes too. "Meerkats . . ."

He loved this place.

He really did.

MORE ABOUT WILD ANIMALS

SPIDER MONKEYS

These are the largest of the monkey groups. They're the only ones that don't have thumbs—maybe with those long tails, they don't need them.

They bark like dogs and neigh like horses.

They're endangered now because their homes in the rain forests are being cleared. They're also hunted for meat. Zoos are helping them stay alive.

GIRAFFES

World Giraffe Day: June 21.

A baby giraffe is called a calf. It runs with its mother when it's only ten hours old.

Giraffes grunt and snort. They snore, hiss, and moo. When the mom whistles for her calf, it mews back.

Every giraffe has different spots. But they all have four stomachs.

In the wild, many babies don't live to grow up. Zoos give them safe places to live.

WHAT MITCHELL LEARNED AT CAMP TO HELP WILDLIFE

1. Keep your cat indoors. Five million birds are killed by outdoor cats every year.

2. Put a birdbath in your yard. Fill it with water every day.

3. Plant a tree for birds to nest.

4. Help clean parks and outdoor spaces.

5. Don't pull dandelions out of your lawn. Bees love them.

READ MORE OF THE

MYSTERIES ON ZOO LANE!